JAY'S QUEST

To order additional copies of this book, contact:
Xlibris Corporation
1-888-795-4274
www.Xlibris.com
Orders@Xlibris.com

This book
is dedicated to the memory of
Harold "PawPaw" Davis

Special thanks to
Rev. Steve Bolen

Kaden

Live Love Laugh

Jay was a young bear
who had a lot of questions.
His questions always led to
explorations.

One day, he wondered what
you could see from the top of a tree.
So he went up the next tree he saw.

On another day, he decided
to see what a frog does all day.
So he followed a frog for almost a day.
He followed the frog everywhere it went.
He decided he was glad to be a bear
and not a frog......too wet!

One morning as he sat
down for breakfast, a different
question came to Jay.
He looked up at his parents
and asked,

"Have you ever seen God?"

His parents thought for a moment.
His mother said "No, I haven't seen
God....not till I get to heaven,
but I know God is there."
Jay finished his breakfast and
thought about what his mother had said.
He wondered how she knew
God was there if she had never seen God.
He needed more information.

As Jay started out of the house,
he saw his sister playing in her room.
He stopped and asked her,
"Jenny, have you ever seen God?"
"No, I don't think so,"
said Jenny....
" Have you seen my teddy bear?
Do you want to play?"
Jay smiled, said no, and went on his way.

As he continued out of the house,
he found his brother playing in the den.
He stopped and asked,
"Ben, have you ever seen God?"
Ben never looked up
from his video game.
"No, but I think God is at the end of this
level...."
Jay headed out on his quest for the day.

As he walked through the woods, Jay found his grandfather in the river

"Hey Paw Paw!"

Jay called as he came out of the woods. He took a seat on a rock and watched his grandfather.

"Paw Paw.....have you ever seen God?"

Paw Paw waded over and took a seat next to Jay.

Paw Paw looked down at Jay and smiled.
"You're looking for God?
Yes, I have seen God.
I see God every day."
Jay was looking around to see if he could see
God too. "Where do you see God?" Jay
asked excitedly!
"Jay, I see God in the sunrise and the moon's
shine. I see God in a bird's flight and in the
storm's might. I see God in everything.
I even see God in you."

It became a part of Jay's day to listen to Paw Paw tell him how he sees God.

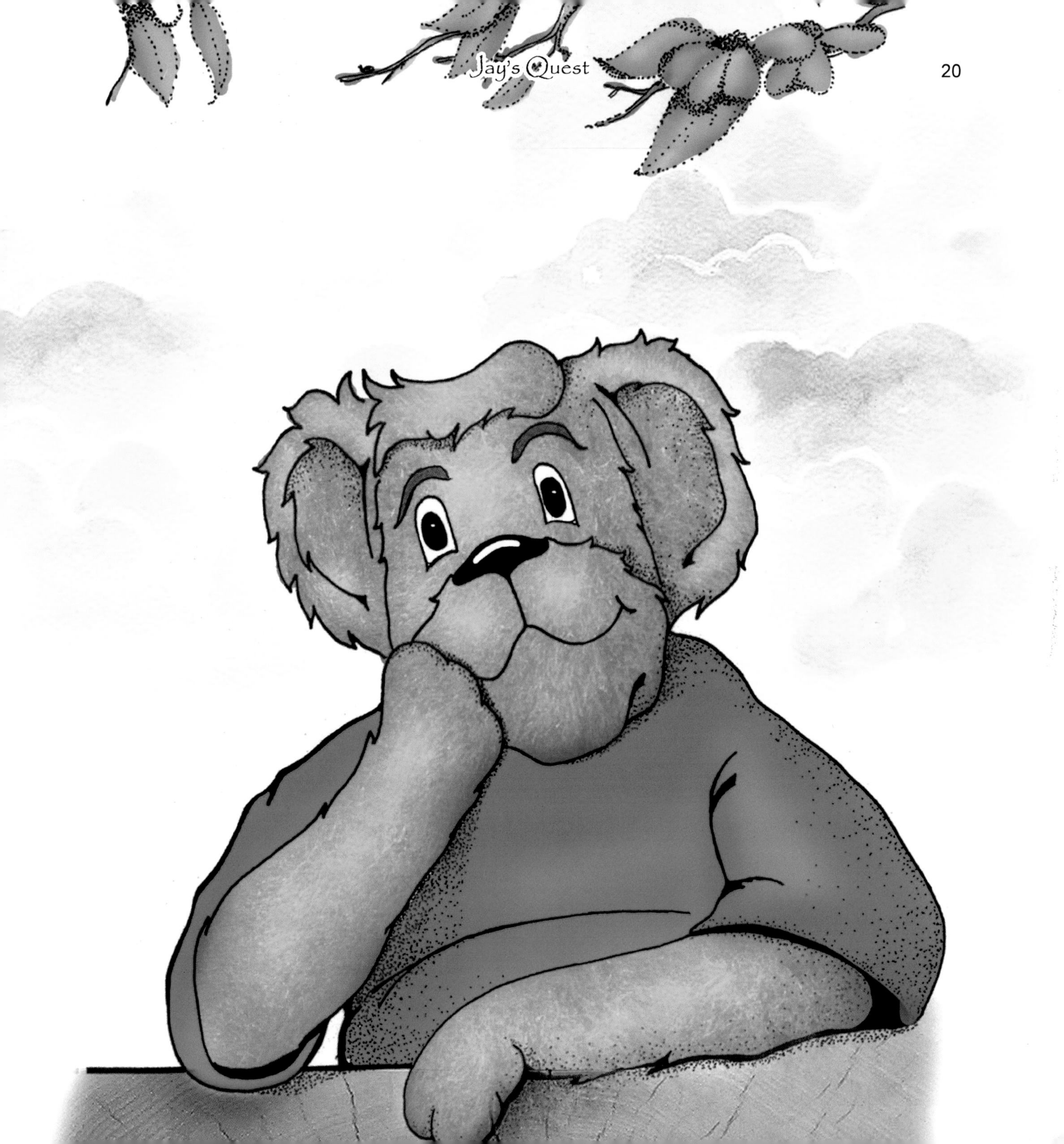

It became a part of Jay's
journey to look for
God every day.

Jay is older now, and
his Paw Paw has
journeyed on.
Jay still explores life, but he
looks at everything
a lot differently, for now
he looks for God
EVERYWHERE!

Edwards Brothers Malloy
Thorofare, NJ USA
February 20, 2013